New, Improved! Dykes To Watch Out For

Also by Alison Bechdel

Dykes To Watch Out For
More Dykes To Watch Out For

New, Improved! Dykes To Watch Out For

by Alison Bechdel

Firebrand Books
Ithaca, New York

Alison Bechdel's cartoons, including those in this collection, appear regularly in more than two dozen newspapers and magazines in the U.S., Canada, and Great Britain.

Book and cover design by Alison Bechdel and Betsy Bayley

Printed in the United States by McNaughton & Gunn

Library of Congress Cataloging-in-Publication Data

Bechdel, Alison.
    New, improved! dykes to watch out for / Alison Bechdel.
        p.   cm.
    ISBN 0–932379–80–X : $16.95. — ISBN 0–932379–79–6 (pbk.) : $7.95
    1. Lesbianism—United States—Caricatures and cartoons.
  2. Lesbians—United States—Caricatures and cartoons.   I. Title.
  II. Title: Dykes to watch out for.
  HQ75.6.U5B424   1990
  305.48'9664—dc20   90–3184
                                                      CIP

Acknowledgments

I would like to thank all the people who have, among other things, given me criticism, offered advice, inspired plot developments, read my rough drafts, psychoanalyzed my characters, bolstered my ego, parodied me, posed for me, shared intimate details of their lives with me, helped think up punch lines, and indulged my favorite pastime of conversing about what will happen next in the strip.

Especially helpful were Lisa Albrecht, Barrie Borich, Trissa Baden, Joan Benson, Susan Denelsbeck, Nikki Feist, Sally Gordon, Nancy Hammond, Nett Hart, Vicki Jedlicka, Judith Katz, Claire Keister, Kris Kovick, Randy Kraemer, Johanna Lee, Bettina Lupion, Alissa Oppenheimer, Kathleen O'Connor, Joan Owen, Emily Rothschild, Flo Solon, and Patricia Elizabeth Winick.

Thanks also to all the wonderful women and men I've met traveling, and all the ones who've written to me, for sharing your remarkable stories.

And to Ethel and Julia, for keeping me company.

And my eternal gratitude to Nancy Bereano of Firebrand Books, who had faith in me from the very, very beginning.

Introducing ...

Mo

A COMMITTED LESBIAN-FEMINIST CULTURAL WORKER (SHE STOCKS SHELVES AT **MADWIMMIN BOOKS**), MO IS CHIEFLY MOTIVATED BY FREE-FLOATING GUILT IN COMBINATION WITH A HYPERSENSITIVE MORAL FIBER. HER INTENTIONS ARE ALWAYS HONORABLE AND HER CLOSEST FRIENDS DESCRIBE HER AS "CHALLENGING."

Virginia

Vanessa

Harriet

TO ALL APPEARANCES EASYGOING AND STABLE, HARRIET IS DEDICATED TO HER CAREER AS A STATE HUMAN RIGHTS INVESTIGATOR. SHE BELIEVES IN TAKING POLITICAL ACTION RATHER THAN WALLOWING IN LIBERAL GUILT, BUT FELL FOR MO ANYWAY.

7

Clarice

Toni

LAW STUDENT WITH A SOUL, CLARICE IS A FIRM BELIEVER IN WORKING FOR CHANGE WITHIN THE SYSTEM. SHE WAS MO'S FIRST LOVER, BUT NOW THEY'RE JUST FRIENDS. CLARICE IS HAPPILY DEVOTED TO HER LONG-TERM RELATIONSHIP WITH TONI... OR **IS** SHE?

TONI IS HELPING TO PUT CLARICE THROUGH LAW SCHOOL WITH HER JOB AS A C.P.A. SHE'S WAITING TILL THE TIME IS RIGHT TO COME OUT AT WORK -- AND TO HER FAMILY. MAYBE AFTER SHE GETS PREGNANT.

Lois

LOIS IS MO'S COWORKER AT THE BOOKSTORE. THEY ARE THE BEST OF FRIENDS DESPITE THE FACT THAT LOIS IS LESS CONCERNED ABOUT STARVATION AND CORRUPTION THAN WITH FLIRTATION AND SEDUCTION. SHE IS NONETHELESS A STAUNCH ADVOCATE OF COLLECTIVE LIVING, AND SHARES A HOUSE WITH GINGER AND SPARROW.

10,000 MANIACS

Ginger

GINGER FIGURES THAT IF SHE **HAS** TO TEACH FRESHMAN ENGLISH, AT LEAST SHE CAN PUT AUDRE LORDE ON THE READING LIST. WHEN SHE'S NOT WORKING ON HER PH.D. OR BATTLING THE UNIVERSITY BUREAUCRACY, SHE WATCHES MTV AND HAS ILL-FATED AFFAIRS.

Digger

Sparrow

BETWEEN HER INDIVIDUAL AND GROUP THERAPY SESSIONS, 12-STEP MEETINGS, CHIROPRACTIC APPOINTMENTS, AND SPIRITUALITY CIRCLES, SPARROW HAS HARDLY ANY TIME LEFT OVER TO GUILT-TRIP HER LESS HIGHLY-EVOLVED HOUSEMATES.

Jezanna

BOSS OF MADWIMMIN BOOKS, A NON-COLLECTIVELY-RUN FEMINIST BOOKSTORE, JEZANNA IS A RECOVERING WORKAHOLIC SHE HOSTS ANNUAL COMING OUT PARTIES AND MAKES VAIN ATTEMPTS TO KEEP LOIS AWAY FROM HER MORE VULNERABLE FRIENDS.

FEMINIST BOOKSTORE NEWS

9

the DILEMMA

24

© 1988 BY ALISON BECHDEL

HAVING DECIDED, UPON FURTHER DISCUSSION, THAT SAFER-SEX PRECAUTIONS WERE NOT **NECESSARY**, MO AND HARRIET PROCEEDED TO INDULGE IN A **WIDE RANGE** OF AMOROUS EXPLORATIONS. SHORTLY AFTERWARDS, WE FIND MO PONDERING HER NEW **NON-CELIBATE** STATUS.

JEEZ, THAT WAS **NICE**... I GUESS I DIDN'T **FORGET HOW** AFTER ALL...

HOW CAN SHE **SLEEP?** I CAN **NEVER** SLEEP IN A STRANGE BED... **OR** WITH A STRANGE **PERSON** FOR THAT MATTER... PARTICULARLY WHEN THEY'RE LYING ON MY **ARM**...

WITH ZEN-LIKE PATIENCE, OUR HEROINE PERSEVERES INTO THE NIGHT AS HER **ARM**, IF NOTHING ELSE, **DOZES OFF.**

...SO **NOW** WHAT? IS THIS JUST A CASUAL **THING** FOR HER? MAYBE SHE DOES THIS ALL THE **TIME**... MAYBE SHE'S **INCAPABLE** OF **COMMITMENT**, OR WORSE YET, **NON-MONOGAMOUS** ON **PRINCIPLE!**

...OR MAYBE SHE THINKS THIS MEANS WE'RE **MARRIED!** WHAT IF SHE STARTS CRITICIZING MY **TABLE MANNERS** AND ASKING ME WHAT I'M **THINKING ABOUT!** I DON'T THINK I'M **READY** FOR THIS...

11

* COMMITTEE IN SOLIDARITY WITH THE PEOPLE OF EL SALVADOR

WHAT'LL **THAT** ACCOMPLISH?! IT'S **RIDICULOUS** THAT REAGAN'S EVEN **ASKING** FOR THIS MONEY! WE SHOULD ALL **DROP** WHAT WE'RE DOING, GO TO D.C., AND **CHAIN** OURSELVES TO THE CAPITOL **DOORS!**

NO, NO, NO... THAT'S JUST **MISDIRECTED ENERGY!** I THINK WE SHOULD ALL HAVE A **MEDITATION** RITUAL AND SEND CONGRESS A HEAVY DOSE OF **WHITE LIGHT!**

AW, SPARROW! DON'T GIVE ME THAT UPPER-MIDDLE CLASS NEW AGE **TWADDLE!** THE ONLY WAY TO EFFECT **CHANGE** IS THROUGH **DIRECT ACTION**, NOT WEARING EXPENSIVE **CRYSTALS** AROUND OUR **NECKS!**

IF YOU THINK ANYONE'S GOING TO **NOTICE**, LET ALONE **CARE**, THAT YOU'VE CHAINED YOURSELF TO A **DOOR**, LOIS, YOU'RE **MISTAKEN!** WE ALL HAVE A RESPONSIBILITY TO THE **DEMOCRATIC PROCESS** TO MAKE OUR **VOTE COUNT!**

THE "DEMOCRATIC PROCESS" IS TOTALLY **DYSFUNCTIONAL!** NOTHING'LL CHANGE UNTIL SOCIETY REALIZES HOW **SICK** IT IS! OUR **FIRST** RESPONSIBILITY IS TO HEAL OURSELVES.... THE **WORLD** WILL **FOLLOW!**

WHY DO WE WASTE OUR ENERGY **FIGHTING** LIKE THIS?

IT'S ANOTHER **F.B.I.** SCHEME. THEY'VE BEEN INJECTING OUR **TOFU** WITH **TESTOSTERONE.**

COMMUNIQUÉ

26

©1988 BY ALISON BECHDEL

A ALTHOUGH SHE IS EXPECTED TO OPEN THE DOORS OF **MADWIMMIN BOOKS** TO THE PUBLIC IN TEN MINUTES, MO IS **UNABLE** TO **WRENCH** HERSELF FROM **HARRIET'S EMBRACES!**

CAN'T YOU CALL **LOIS** AND HAVE HER OPEN UP FOR YOU?

NO, NOT **LOIS**! SHE SAW US LAST NIGHT AND SHE'D **KNOW** WHY I WAS LATE.

SO?

SO KNOWING **LOIS**, IT'LL BE ALL OVER **TOWN** BY **NOON**. I'LL CALL **ARIADNE**. SHE OWES ME A FAVOR.

HI, GINGER. IT'S ARIADNE. I HAFTA **CANCEL** OUR **BRUNCH** DATE. I'M WORKING FOR **MO** THIS MORNING. NO, I DUNNO... SHE JUST SAID 'SOMETHING CAME UP.'

LESBIAN BED DEATH
JOAN HOOLIHAN

MORNING GINGER!

HI, NAOMI! **SAY**, GUESS WHO DIDN'T SHOW UP FOR **WORK** THIS MORNING AFTER WE SAW HER AT THE **TOPAZ** WITH **HARRIET** LAST NIGHT... METHINKS THE CHASTE MAIDEN **MO** FINALLY GOT **LAID**!

14

...ORGANIC BLACK BEANS $1.55...

HEY, TONI.. DIDJA HEAR ABOUT **MO & HARRIET**?

HONEY! I PICKED UP SOME **HOT NEWS** AT THE **CO-OP!**

SO SUE ME

NIGHT COURT

IMPOSING LEGAL TOME VOL IXI —FROWST

HEY, **LOIS!** GUESS WHO FINALLY **DID IT!**

DAMN.

MEANWHILE, MO **TEARS** HERSELF AWAY...

MMM... -SMAK- WE HAFTA STOP...

YEAH, I KNOW -SLURP- I'LL BE LATE **AGAIN.**

AND ARRIVES AT THE **BOOKSTORE** BY NOON, JUST AS **LOIS** DROPS IN!

♪HEL-LO, MO!♪ YOU LOOK **FLUSHED.** 'JA **WORK OUT** THIS MORNING OR SOMETHING? Y'KNOW, I COULD REALLY GET **INTO** AN EXERCISE PROGRAM LIKE **YOURS!**

GREAT, LOIS. **GREAT.** I'M REALLY **IMPRESSED.** I THINK THIS COMMUNITY JUST SET THE LAND SPEED **RECORD** FOR **GOSSIP MONGERING!**

DETAILS! I WANT **DETAILS!**

15

A Little Domestic

© 1988 BY ALISON BECHDEL

27

OH, NO! ANOTHER ONE!

WHAT?! A COLLECTION NOTICE? A CHAIN LETTER?

NO. A WEDDING INVITATION FROM AN OLD STRAIGHT FRIEND.

I DUNNO, MO. I CAN'T QUITE PICTURE YOU IN PEACH TAFFETA... WHAT'LL YOU WEAR?

DON'T BE SILLY, HARRIET! I CAN'T GO. I'M GONNA MISS OLE' SUZANNE, THOUGH.

WHERE'S SHE GOING?

NOWHERE. BUT SHE WON'T SPEAK TO ME AFTER I TELL HER IT'S AGAINST MY PRINCIPLES TO COLLUDE WITH INSTITUTIONALIZED PATRIARCHY BY CONGRATULATING HER OR BY TAKING PART IN THE CEREMONY.

I DON'T GET IT. SO SHE WANTS TO GET MARRIED. WHAT'S THAT TO YOU?

16

18

DON'T **GUILT-TRIP** ME, LOIS. YOU'RE NOT THE **ONLY** ONE TRYING TO SAVE THE WORLD. BUT IF YOU WANT TO DO SOMETHING **TRULY** RADICAL, THEN TRY **THERAPY.**

THERAPY IS A **SELF-INDULGENT, CLASSIST, INDIVIDUAL SOLUTION!**

THAT'S EXACTLY WHAT I'D **EXPECT** TO HEAR FROM SOMEONE WHO'S NEVER EVEN **TRIED** IT. PSYCHOTHERAPY IS A TOOL FOR ACHIEVING REAL **AUTONOMY** AND **EMPOWERMENT...**

... SO WE CAN OVERCOME THE **REPRESSION** IMPOSED ON US BY THE **PATRIARCHY.** YOU CAN'T GET MUCH MORE **REVOLUTIONARY** THAN **THAT.**

I DON'T NEED TO PAY A **SHRINK** TO GET **EMPOWERED!** AND BESIDES, I'M PERFECTLY **HEALTHY** EMOTIONALLY!

UH-HUH, **RIGHT.** THAT'S WHY YOU SLEEP WITH EVERY WOMAN YOU **MEET.** FACE IT, **LOIS!** YOU'RE A **SEX ADDICT!**

AT LEAST IT'S **CHEAPER** THAN BEING A **THERAPY JUNKIE!**

I THINK WE SHOULD CONTINUE THIS DISCUSSION WHEN WE'RE BOTH MORE **RATIONAL.** I'M GOING TO **WORK.**

SURE! RUN AWAY FROM A LITTLE **HONEST CONFLICT!** GO **PROCESS** IT WITH YOUR **GROUP!** AND DON'T EXPECT ME TO SAVE YOU ANY **TURNIP LOAF!**

21

22

JEEZ, TONI! I'M STILL IN **SCHOOL**! WE DON'T HAVE ANY MONEY... OR ANY **SPERM**, FOR THAT MATTER... WE CAN'T RUSH **INTO** ANYTHING!

AND WE CAN'T WAIT TILL WE'RE **MILLIONAIRES** TO HAVE A BABY, EITHER! YOU'LL BE OUT OF SCHOOL EVENTUALLY. WE'LL LOOK FOR A SPERM DONOR OR GO TO A CLINIC.

BUT WHERE WOULD WE **PUT** A BABY? WHAT IF WE WANTED TO **TRAVEL**? WHAT IF WE JUST WANTED TO GO TO A **MOVIE**? OUR LIVES WOULD NEVER BE THE **SAME**!

THAT'S PART OF THE **IDEA**. I LOVE YOU VERY **MUCH**, CLARICE! I THINK WE HAVE A LOT TO **OFFER** A KID!

I DUNNO, HONEY... I GUESS DEEP **DOWN**, PART OF ME THINKS LESBIANS WERE CREATED FOR **OTHER** PURPOSES THAN RAISING **CHILDREN**!

LIKE **WHAT**? BEING **DRILL SERGEANTS** OR **DOG BREEDERS**?! THAT'S DOWNRIGHT **HOMOPHOBIC**, CLARICE!

UH... I **MEANT**... DON'T YOU THINK WE SHOULD WAIT TILL I'VE DONE SOME **THERAPY**? HOW CAN I BECOME SOMEONE'S **MOTHER** UNTIL I RESOLVE MY **OWN** CHILDHOOD?!

IF I DIDN'T **KNOW** YOU BETTER, CLARICE, I'D SAY YOU WERE **SCARED**.

TRY **MAD** WITH **TERROR**.

23

ONE AFTERNOON IN THE

GROVES OF ACADEME

© 1988 BY ALISON BECHDEL

31

PLANNING HAS BEGUN FOR THE ANNUAL GAY & LESBIAN STUDIES CONFERENCE.

COMMITTEES HAVE BEEN FORMED.

CLARICE IS ON HER WAY TO THE FIRST MEETING OF THE ACCESSIBILITY COMMITTEE.

GINGER, GRADUATE STUDENT IN ENGLISH, LEAVES HER SECTION OF FRESHMEN WITH SOME WORDS OF WISDOM...

QUIT WHINING! READING SOMETHING BY SOMEONE WHO'S NOT STRAIGHT, WHITE, & MALE IS **NOT** GOING TO **KILL**YOU!

AND SETS OUT FOR THE VERY SAME MEETING.

24

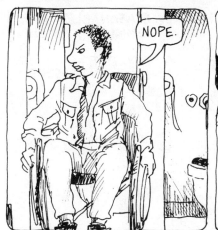

TROUBLE in Paradise

©1988 BY ALISON BECHDEL

32

A **AFTER A GRUELING DAY AT WORK AND SCHOOL, OUR DYNAMIC DUO REGROUPS FOR DINNER AT THE TOPAZ.**

LOOK, CHICA! THERE'S A GROUP OF **LESBIANS** MEETING TO TALK ABOUT HAVING **BABIES**. LET'S GO! MAYBE IT WILL HELP YOU TO FEEL LESS **SCARED**.

UH...**GROUP**?

CLASSIFIEDS

EVERY TUESDAY NIGHT AT THE COMMUNITY CENTER.

OH, **TOO** BAD. TUESDAYS ARE THE **COMMITTEE** NIGHTS FOR THE GAY AND LESBIAN STUDIES CONFERENCE.

OH, OF **COURSE.** HOW **SILLY** OF ME TO THINK PLANNING A **BABY** COULD TAKE PRIORITY OVER PLANNING A FOUR-DAY **CONFERENCE.**

TONI, BE **REASONABLE!** I'VE ALREADY **COMMITTED** MYSELF TO THIS! AND I **DO** WANT US TO HAVE A BABY, BUT I CAN'T STAND THIS CONSTANT **PRESSURE!**

Café Topaz

OPEN

27

FATAL ATTRACTION

33

© 1988 BY ALISON BECHDEL

TONI IS MAKING A SUDDEN TRIP TO **SAN JUAN** FOR HER GRANDMOTHER'S **FUNERAL.**

THE **WORST** THING IS, MY ABUELITA WAS THE ONLY **SANE** MEMBER OF MY ENTIRE **FAMILY.**

I KNOW, HONEY. CALL ME IF THEY START TO DRIVE YOU CRAZY. I WISH I COULD COME **WITH** YOU.

GATE **78**

THAT EVENING, CLARICE ATTENDS A MEETING OF THE **ACCESSIBILITY COMMITTEE.**

WE STILL NEED ANOTHER SIGN-LANGUAGE INTERPRETER FOR THE PANEL DISCUSSION, "**LESBIANS AND GAYMEN WORKING TOGETHER; TACTICAL TEAM OR TOTAL TRAVESTY?**"

NO, WE DON'T. MARIA SAID **SHE** COULD DO IT.

BUT WE ALREADY **HAVE** A WOMAN SIGNING. WE NEED A **MAN** FOR **PARITY,** ESPECIALLY ON **THIS** PANEL!

MATTERS DRAG ON...

BUT WE ONLY **HAVE** ONE MALE INTERPRETER, AND HE'S DOING THE MEN-**ONLY** WORKSHOP, "**SENSUAL, SALACIOUS, & SAFE**" IN THE SAME TIME-SLOT!

FRIENDLY ADVICE

34

© 1988 BY ALISON BECHDEL

I'M GLAD YOU COULD COME OVER, MO. I REALLY NEED TO **TALK** TO YOU... UH... WHAT WOULD YOU THINK IF I HAD AN **AFFAIR** WITH **GINGER**?

WHAT?

I'M SO **ATTRACTED** TO HER! I CAN'T **DESCRIBE** IT... IT'S LIKE... GRAVITY... FATE... **DESTINY**!

WHAT?!

SHE FEELS THE SAME TOWARD ME. WE TALKED ABOUT IT LAST NIGHT.

CLARICE, WHAT ABOUT **TONI**?

WHAT **ABOUT** HER? THIS HAS **NOTHING** TO **DO** WITH MY COMMITMENT TO **TONI!** IN FACT, I THINK IT WOULD BE **UNHEALTHY** FOR OUR RELATIONSHIP IF I **DIDN'T** ACT ON THESE FEELINGS FOR GINGER! **BESIDES**, TONI'S STILL IN PUERTO RICO.

WHOA, CLARICE... **CLARICE?** ARE YOU **IN** THERE, OR HAVE YOU BEEN **POSSESSED** BY AN **ALIEN?**

CLOSE·EN·COUNTER

© 1988 BY ALISON BECHDEL

A TIP O' THE NIB TO PAT WINICK

35

HEEDLESS OF THEIR FRIENDS' ADVICE, CLARICE AND GINGER FIND THEMSELVES AT THE **POINT** OF **NO** RETURN.

WANNA COME **IN?** LOIS AND SPARROW WON'T BE HOME TILL **LATE.**

SURE.

IGNORE THE MESS. IT'S MY **THESIS.**

WHAT'S IT **ABOUT?**

IT'S ABOUT **HISTORICAL TRENDS** IN DOMINANT-CULTURE **CRITICISM** OF **AFRO·AMERICAN** LITERATURE...

... WITH A FOCUS ON THE CRITICAL RESPONSE TO THE INFLUENCE ... UH ..

... OF THE **ORAL TRADITION** IN, UM... CONTEMPORARY FICTION BY BLACK WOMEN... MMM..

SMAK

TWO HOURS AND FIFTEEN MINUTES LATER...

OOPS! 'SCUSE ME!

I HOPE YOU KNOW WHAT YOU'RE GETTING **INTO**, GINGER, THAT'S ALL **I** HAVE TO SAY.

SLAM!

GINGER... I HAVE TO LEAVE IN CASE TONI CALLS IN THE MORNING... UM... I HAD A **GREAT** TIME.

ME TOO. YOU BUSY TOMORROW?

UH... YEAH. TONI'S FLIGHT GETS IN AT 6.

ARE YOU GOING TO **TELL** HER?

TELL HER **WHAT?**

HAS CLARICE BEEN POSSESSED BY AN **ALIEN?** WHAT'S GOING **ON** HERE, ANYWAY?! DON'T TOUCH THAT **DIAL!**

33

In the HEAT of the NIGHT

© 1988 BY ALISON BECHDEL

36

IT'S BEDTIME AT HARRIET'S APARTMENT...

I JUST CAN'T BELIEVE IT! WHY IS CLARICE DOING THIS?

I DON'T KNOW! SHE AND TONI SEEMED SO HAPPY!

THEY'RE MY ROLE MODELS, HARRIET! DON'T THEY REALIZE THEY HAVE A RESPONSIBILITY TO ME TO STAY TOGETHER?!

MO, STOP. IT'S TOO HOT TO RAVE.

THAT'S IT! IT'S THE GREENHOUSE EFFECT! THIS OPPRESSIVE HEAT IS CAUSING HORMONAL IMBALANCES AND CLARICE IS ONE OF THE FIRST VICTIMS!

I MEAN, DOESN'T IT BOTHER YOU, HARRIET? TO SEE AN ESTABLISHED, LONG-TERM LESBIAN RELATIONSHIP -- ONE THAT YOU LOOK TO FOR EXAMPLE AND INSPIRATION -- TO SEE IT JUST BITE THE DUST?!

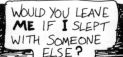

THE IN-TERRO-GATION

37

© 1988 BY ALISON BECHDEL

CLARICE HAS JUST PICKED TONI UP AT THE AIRPORT.

SO, DID YOU HAVE **FUN** WHILE I WAS GONE? ANY WILD **AFFAIRS**?

WHAAAT?!

SWERVE!

SCREEE

RELAX! JEEZ, I WAS JUST **KIDDING** SWEETHEART!

SORRY! I... UH... SO HOW WAS IT SEEING YOUR **FAMILY**?

PRETTY BAD. WITH MY GRANDMOTHER GONE, THERE WAS NO ONE TO STOP THEM ALL PESTERING ME ABOUT WHEN I'M GETTING **MARRIED**. THE FUNERAL WAS A CIRCUS.

AIRPORT

YEAH, I CAN IMAGINE. I'M SORRY.

CLARICE, WHAT'S **WRONG**? YOU HAVE THE STEERING WHEEL IN A **DEATH GRIP!**

TONI... I WENT OUT WITH **GINGER** LAST NIGHT.

I REMEMBER, YOU MADE A DATE FOR **COFFEE**. SO?

36

37

...And Nothing But The Truth

38

© 1988 BY ALISON BECHDEL

OF **COURSE** NOT! I DON'T WANT TO GET IN THE MIDDLE OF **THIS!**

IT'S **WEIRD**... I CAN'T IMAGINE CLARICE WOULDN'T HAVE **TOLD** HER!

I DUNNO... IT'S NOT LIKE SHE'S **LYING** EXACTLY... AFTER ALL, IT **IS TRUE** THAT THEY **KISSED**... YEAH, **THAT'S IT!**

IT'S **LAW SCHOOL**, LOIS! I **KNEW** THEY'D GET HER EVENTUALLY!

HALF-TRUTHS! LOOPHOLES! CHALK UP ANOTHER VICTIM TO THE **UNSCRUPULOUS, MACHIAVELLIAN CLUTCHES** OF THE **LEGAL MENTALITY!**

YEAH, RIGHT. WILL YOU CALM **DOWN?** WHATEVER IT IS, **SOMEONE'S** GOT TO **TALK** TO HER.

GULP!

39

Naturally Resourceful

39

© 1988 By Alison Bechdel

I'M TOO EXHAUSTED TO EVEN **THINK** OF COOKING. WHAT WOULD WE DO WITHOUT **TAKE-OUT** FOOD?

HM... WELL, FOR **ONE** THING, WE'D HAVE LESS OF THESE **STYROFOAM CONTAINERS** CLUTTERING UP THE ENVIRONMENT!

LOOKIT THIS! YOU CAN'T **RECYCLE** IT. IT HAS A **HALF-LIFE** OF A **ZILLION YEARS!**

DID YOU KNOW, WHEN THEY **MAKE** ONE OF THESE THINGS, SOME **OZONE-DESTROYING CHEMICAL** IS RELEASED INTO THE ATMOSPHERE?

WITHOUT **OZONE** TO SCREEN ULTRA-VIOLET **RADIATION**, THE EARTH'S **TEMPERATURE** IS RISING... THAT'S WHY WE'VE BEEN HAVING RECORD **HEAT WAVES** AND A **DROUGHT.**

THIS IS THE **BEGINNING** OF THE **END**, HARRIET! **GLOBAL ECOLOGICAL DISASTER** IS UPON US!

41

The BIG PICTURE

©1988
40
BY ALISON BECHDEL

On a long walk with Clarice, Mo relies on her inborn **TACT** and adroit **INTERPERSONAL SKILLS** to broach a **DELICATE SUBJECT**...

So, Clarice... when do you plan to tell Toni you **CHEATED** on her while she was **OUT** of **TOWN**?

WHAT?! I didn't "**CHEAT**" on her, Mo! And **BESIDES**, it's **NONE** of your @#&*☺! **BUSINESS**!

Well, I wish it **WASN'T**.. but this is a small community, and like it or not, other people **KNOW** what's going **ON**. It's just not **FAIR** that Toni **DOESN'T**.

Oh, Mo... she's so **HURT** and **UPSET** thinking Ginger and I just **KISSED**... I **CAN'T** tell her we **SLEPT** together!

LISTEN, Clarice. Given the speed **NEWS** travels in this town, she'll find out **SOON** whether **YOU** tell her or **NOT**.

I KNOW... I have to **TELL** her. (sniff) Oh, jeez, she'll never (sob) **TRUST** me **AGAIN**! What a **MESS**!

You can say **THAT** again!

43

Jezanna throws down

The Gauntlet

© 1988 BY ALISON BECHDEL

41

SAY, MO, I'M HAVING A **COMING-OUT PARTY** IN A COUPLE WEEKS AND I'D LIKE YOU TO COME.

A **COMING-OUT** PARTY? SOMEHOW I NEVER FIGURED YOU FOR THE **DEBUTANTE TYPE**, JEZANNA...

VERY FUNNY. YOU KNOW WHAT I MEAN. "**COMING OUT**" AS IN TELLING PEOPLE YOU'RE A **LESBIAN**.

MADWIMMIN BOOKS

OPEN

BUT I ALREADY **KNOW** YOU'RE A LESBIAN.

MO, IT'S A GOOD THING I HIRED YOU FOR YOUR **STUNNING GOOD LOOKS** AND NOT YOUR **KEEN WIT** OR **PIERCING INTELLECT**. HAVEN'T YOU HEARD ABOUT NATIONAL **COMING-OUT DAY**?

BOOKS

OF **COURSE** I HAVE. I WAS JUST **TEASING** YOU. DID YOU REALLY HIRE ME FOR MY **LOOKS**?

NO. SO, THE IDEA IS, EVERYONE TAKES THE NEXT STEP IN THEIR **COMING OUT PROCESS.** THEN AT MY PARTY WE CAN **CELEBRATE** AND SHARE OUR **STORIES.**

THE **NEXT STEP**, HUH? GEE, I'M OUT TO PRACTICALLY EVERYONE I **KNOW**...

YEAH? HOW DO YOUR **PARENTS** DEAL WITH IT?

UH... MY **PARENTS**?

DON'T **TELL** ME MS. **POLITICAL CORRECT-NESS** INCARNATE ISN'T **OUT** TO HER OWN **PARENTS!**

I KNOW, I KNOW. I'M PERPETU-ATING MY OWN INTERNALIZED **HOMOPHOBIA** AS WELL AS THAT OF MY **FAMILY** AND **SOCIETY** AT LARGE. **COMING OUT** IS THE MOST **EFFECTIVE TOOL** WE **HAVE** AGAINST THIS CULTURE'S **FEAR, SHAME,** AND **MISCON-CEPTIONS** ABOUT **HOMOSEXUALITY.**

YOU CERTAINLY HAVE THE **RAP** DOWN. WHY NOT TELL YOUR **FOLKS** THE GOOD NEWS?

BECAUSE I'M **SCARED SHITLESS.**

THAT'S WHY I'M HAVING A **PARTY!** WE'LL ALL BE THERE TO **SUPPORT** EACH OTHER AFTER WE'VE **TOLD** WHOEVER WE'RE GONNA **TELL!**

OKAY, OKAY. YOU'RE RIGHT. I'LL **TELL** THEM. **WHO KNOWS?** MAYBE **THEY'RE** GAY TOO.

ATTA GIRL.

47

Familiar TERMS 43

© 1988 BY ALISON BECHDEL

AT JEZANNA'S COMING OUT PARTY...

"...SO I'M WATCHING **TV** WITH MY FAMILY AND MY **UNCLE** SAYS "THOSE GODDAMN QUEERS **DESERVE** TO GET AIDS." "**INCLUDING ME, UNCLE CARL?!!** " I YELL. YOU COULDA HEARD A **POTATO CHIP** DROP!

"...WHEN I TOLD MY MOM I WAS A **DYKE**, SHE ASKED IF I KNEW ANY NICE **OLDER WOMEN** I COULD FIX HER UP WITH...

SO MO! HOW'D IT GO?

OH, WELL... JEEZ. NOTHING **DRAMATIC**, REALLY. I MEAN, THEY DIDN'T OFFER TO JOIN ME ON THE NEXT **GAY PRIDE** MARCH, BUT THEY DIDN'T SEND A **DEPROGRAMMER** AFTER ME EITHER.

I KNOW WHAT YOU **MEAN.** SOMETIMES I WISH MY PARENTS WOULD GO AHEAD AND THREATEN ME WITH **DAMNATION** INSTEAD OF THE WAY THEY AVOID ANY DISCUSSION OF MY **PERSONAL LIFE.**

ISN'T THAT A **DRAG?** I'M OUT TO MY PARENTS, AND THEY HAVE NO INTEREST IN MY LIFE **AT ALL.** THEY WON'T EVEN ASK ME HOW I'M **DOING**... I GUESS THEY'RE SCARED I'LL SAY "OH, **MOM, DAD!** I'VE BEEN HAVING THE **BEST** CUNNILINGUS!"

JUST DESSERTS

44

©1988 BY ALISON BECHDEL

On the rare occasion of their all having nothing **BETTER** to do, our housemates **GINGER, LOIS, & SPARROW** **SPEND** AN **EVENING** together.

WHAT A ROTTEN MOVIE. WANNA GET SOME DESSERT?

SURE.

OK, BUT I JUST WANT SOME TEA.

Let them Eat Cake

I'LL HAVE A CHOCOLATE **ORGASM** AND A CUP OF COFFEE.

UH...I'LL HAVE THE TRIPLE TASMANIAN DEVILSFOOD **DELIGHT** AND AN ESPRESSO.

MINT TEA AND A **BRAN** MUFFIN, PLEASE.

I THOUGHT YOU WERE **OFF CAFFEINE,** GINGER!

AND I THOUGHT **YOU** WERE ALLERGIC TO **CHOCOLATE.**

I DON'T KNOW **WHY** YOU GUYS **EAT** THIS STUFF IF YOU **KNOW** IT'S **BAD** FOR YOU! DON'T COMPLAIN TO **ME** ABOUT YOUR **HEAD-ACHES** AND **INSOMNIA.**

A SHORT WHILE LATER...

SO GINGER, I HAVEN'T RUN INTO **CLARICE** IN OUR BATH-ROOM LATELY...WHAT'S UP?

WE'RE NOT SEEING EACH OTHER...TURNS OUT SHE SLIGHTLY **EXAGGERATED** HOW NONMONOGAMOUS HER SCENE WITH **TONI** IS.

50

AW, GINGER, THAT'S TOO BAD... I'M SORRY. IN FACT, I'M **SO** SORRY THAT I WILL NOBLY REFRAIN FROM SAYING ' **I TOLD** YOU SO.'

YEAH, YEAH. I KNOW. BUT I DON'T HAVE ANY **REGRETS**. LIKE I TOLD YOU, I JUST WANTED TO **SLEEP** WITH HER, NOT GET **MARRIED**.

UH-OH! **LOOK OUT!** IT'S **GINGER**, WOMAN OF **STEEL**... AND SHE'S **INVULNERABLE!** C'MON, **ADMIT** IT! YOU'RE **HURT!** CAN I HAVE ANOTHER **TEENSY** TASTE OF YOUR CAKE **?**

ACTUALLY, I'M KIND OF **RELIEVED** IT DIDN'T WORK OUT. I'M **SICK** & **TIRED** OF ROMANTIC MELODRAMA. THERE ARE **OTHER** THINGS TO LIFE, AFTER ALL.

YOUR PROBLEM, GINGER, IS THAT YOU'VE NEVER WORKED THROUGH YOUR BREAK-UP WITH **PHYLLIS**. YOU SHOULD JOIN A **THERAPY** GROUP. ARE YOU GONNA **FINISH** THAT, LO?

TAKE IT. I'M STARTING TO **HALLUCINATE**.

URP

SPARROW, YOU WOULD RECOMMEND A THERAPY GROUP IF I HAD **HEMOR-RHOIDS!** NOPE, I'M GOING TO TRY SOME GOOD OLD-FASHIONED **CELIBACY** AND FINISH MY **THESIS!**

YOU **TELL** HER, GINGER! C'MON, WE BETTER HURRY HOME BEFORE WE **CRASH!**

YEAH, I FEEL KINDA **SPEEDY**... D'YOU THINK THEY PUT **SUGAR** IN THE BRAN MUFFINS HERE?

51

53

WHY SHOULD I BE A PRODUCTIVE MEMBER OF A SOCIETY THAT THRIVES BY OPPRESSING EVERYONE ELSE IN THE WORLD?

Y'KNOW, YOU'RE ABSOLUTELY RIGHT! I THINK YOU'VE HIT ON A VERY SYMBOLIC FORM OF PROTEST HERE!

YES! AS A CITIZEN OF A PRIVILEGED COUNTRY, RENOUNCE THE POWER YOU HAVE TO ACTIVELY DISSENT AND EDUCATE! JUST STAY IN BED! THAT'LL SHOW THOSE REPUBLICANS A THING OR TWO.

WHAT A MEANINGFUL WAY TO EXPRESS YOUR SOLIDARITY WITH THE PEOPLE WHO ARE SLEEPING FIVE TO A MATTRESS IN REFUGEE CAMPS AND SHANTYTOWNS AND PRISONS! CAN I GET YOU ANOTHER BLANKET BEFORE I LEAVE?

ALL RIGHT, ALL RIGHT! I'M UP ALREADY!

WHATEVER HAPPENED TO BRIBING YOUR LOVER OUT OF BED WITH HOT BLUEBERRY MUFFINS?

SMAK!

55

MO & LOIS INDULGE IN A SPOT OF

girl talk

© 1988 BY ALISON BECHDEL (47)

SO HOW ARE YOU AND HARRIET DOING? DO I HEAR **WEDDING BELLS?**

WEDDING BELLS? ACTUALLY, LOIS, I'M NOT SURE **WHAT** WE'RE DOING! I MEAN, WE SEE EACH OTHER 3 OR **4** NIGHTS A WEEK ... WE HAVE **GREAT SEX** ... SHE HAS A **TOOTHBRUSH** AT MY HOUSE ...

WHAT DO YOU **CALL** THAT? **GOING STEADY?** A **FLING?** I DUNNO!

WELL ... ARE YOU **IN LOVE?**

IN **LOVE?!** JEEZ, LOIS! I MEAN ... WHAT **IS** LOVE, ANYWAY?

C'MON, MO! YOU'VE BEEN GOING OUT FOR ALMOST A **YEAR!** YOU'VE NEVER SAID YOU **LOVE** EACH OTHER?

LOVE IS SERIOUS **STUFF,** LOIS! IF I DON'T KNOW WHAT IT **MEANS,** HOW CAN I TELL HARRIET I **LOVE** HER?

I DUNNO! DOESN'T IT JUST **SLIP OUT?!**

YOU MIGHT SAY IT ON THE FIRST DATE, LOIS, BUT TO **ME** IT **MEANS** SOMETHING!

PARDONNEZ MOI, YOUR HOLINESS! PLEASE EXCUSE MY **MORAL INFERIORITY!**

AW, LOIS, **I'M** SORRY... I KNOW WHAT YOU MEAN. IT ALMOST **HAS** SLIPPED OUT A COUPLE TIMES. I GUESS I'M **SCARED.** I WANT TO TELL HER AT THE **RIGHT MOMENT,** Y'KNOW?

TELL HER IN A SULTRY WHISPER WHILE YOU'RE LICKING THE **CROOK** OF HER **KNEE. THAT'S** ALWAYS A GOOD MOMENT.

NO, I DON'T WANT TO TELL HER WHILE WE'RE HAVING **SEX**...IT'S ABOUT SO MUCH **MORE** THAN THAT.

FINE! TELL HER WHILE YOU'RE CHANGING THE **KITTY LITTER!** WHAT ARE YOU **AFRAID** OF? I MEAN, WHAT'S THE WORST THING THAT COULD **HAPPEN?**

THE **WORST?** SHE GRABS HER **TOOTHBRUSH** AND RUNS **SCREAMING** FROM THE **APARTMENT.** OR, **NO!** EVEN **WORSE** THAN THAT,... SHE WHIPS OUT HER **DATEBOOK** AND SAYS WOULDN'T **JUNE** BE A NICE TIME FOR OUR **COMMITMENT CEREMONY!**

58

59

61

POETIC LICENSE

50

© 1989 BY ALISON BECHDEL

Lois ACCOMPANIES GINGER TO A READING BY A RENOWNED LESBIAN **POET** AT THE UNIVERSITY.

◇

WHY AM I **DOING** THIS?! I **HATE** POETRY! I MUST BE REALLY **BORED!**

YOU'RE SUCH A **PHILISTINE,** LOIS! A LITTLE CULTURE WILL DO YOU GOOD!

YEAH, SURE. SITTING AROUND WITH A BUNCHA **PSEUDO-INTELLECTUALS** PRETENDING TO UNDERSTAND WHAT SOME **WACKO POET** IS **EMOTING** ABOUT HAS ALWAYS BEEN **MY** IDEA OF A GOOD TIME!

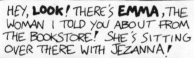

HEY, **LOOK!** THERE'S **EMMA,** THE WOMAN I TOLD YOU ABOUT FROM THE BOOKSTORE! SHE'S SITTING OVER THERE WITH JEZANNA!

SHHH! IT'S STARTING!

I LICK THE DELICATE PEARL...

SHE'S MARRIED TO A **MAN,** BUT JEZANNA SAYS SHE'S JUST COMING OUT! ISN'T SHE **HOT?!**

DO YOU **MIND?!** SOME OF US CAME TO **LISTEN!**

...OF YOUR NAVEL / THE EXPANSE OF YOUR BELLY / A BEACH AT DAWN...

TIGHTASS ACADEMICS!

MAYBE I CAN MAKE SOME **EYE** CONTACT.

...YOUR DESIRE A TIDAL POOL...

WHOA! SHE'S... SHE'S STARING RIGHT **AT ME! CAREFUL,** LOIS, DON'T LOSE YOUR **COOL!**

...RIPE, LIQUID CORAL...

OMIGOD! WAS THAT A **WINK?!** DID SHE REALLY JUST **WINK** AT ME?

...AS THE WAVES CREST, SUBSIDE...

... LAP / AT THE EDGE. THE LINGERING SCENT / OF SEAWEED.

WELL, YOU CAN'T CALL **THAT** POEM DRY AND **INTELLECTUAL!** SHE HAS A WAY OF REALLY BRINGING HER SUBJECT **ALIVE,** DON'T YOU THINK?

I DIDN'T HEAR A WORD SHE SAID... BUT MY OPINION OF POETRY READINGS HAS DEFINITELY **IMPROVED.**

CLAP! CLAP CLAP! CLAP CLEP!

63

A very warm Reception

51

© 1989 BY ALISON BECHDEL

Excited by a steamy bout of **OCULAR FLIRTATION** during a poetry reading, Lois seeks out her **INAMORATA** at the **RECEPTION** afterwards.

THERE SHE IS! WITH JEZANNA OVER BY THE WINE & CHEESE! C'MON!

LOIS, YOU SAID JEZANNA TOLD YOU TO LEAVE THIS WOMAN ALONE! I DON'T THINK SHE'S GONNA TAKE KINDLY TO YOU **FORCING** YOURSELF ON THEM!

SIGN IT 'TO LORNA WITH LOVE'

LEAVE THIS TO ME, GINGER.

JEZANNA! HI! FANCY MEETING **YOU** HERE! YOU KNOW MY HOUSEMATE GINGER, DON'T YOU?

OH. HI, GINGER. HI LOIS. I NEVER THOUGHT I'D SEE **YOU** AT A POETRY READING.

WELL JEZ, I THINK IT'S ALWAYS IMPORTANT TO **TRY NEW EXPERIENCES**... IT KEEPS LIFE **EXCITING**, DON'T YOU AGREE?

I DON'T BELIEVE WE'VE **MET**! I'M LOIS!

CHARMED. I'M EMMA. DON'T YOU WORK WITH JEZANNA? I'VE SEEN YOU AT THE BOOKSTORE.

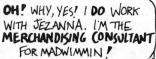

OH! WHY, YES! I DO WORK WITH JEZANNA. I'M THE **MERCHANDISING CONSULTANT** FOR MADWIMMIN!

MERCHANDISING CONSULTANT?! LOIS, YOU'RE A **CLERK**! LISTEN, EMMA, I REALLY HAVE TO GET HOME AND WALK MY DOG. LET'S GO!

OKAY. LET ME JUST FINISH THIS. I'LL BE RIGHT THERE.

SO YOU'RE A **CLERK**! THAT MUST BE **FASCINATING**!

OH! WELL,...IT HAS ITS MOMENTS. UM...WHAT DO **YOU** DO?

I'M A **CHEMICAL DEPENDENCY** COUNSELOR.

OH! UM...I'M **NOT** AN **ALCOHOLIC**... I JUST HAVE A GLASS OF WINE NOW AND THEN AT, YOU KNOW, **RECEPTIONS** AND THINGS!

DON'T WORRY. I WON'T **ARREST** YOU. THAT'S A **LOVELY** EARRING YOU'RE WEARING.

EMMA! I **HATE** TO DRAG YOU **AWAY** LIKE THIS, BUT IF WE DON'T LEAVE RIGHT **NOW**, I'LL HAVE TO FACE **FIFI'S REVENGE**. NICE SEEING YOU, GINGER! G'NIGHT!

I'LL SEE **YOU** AT WORK TOMORROW. WE HAVE SOME **SERIOUS CONSULTING** TO DO.

65

The Wager

52

© 1989 BY ALISON BECHDEL

JEZANNA, THE MORE YOU TELL LOIS TO STAY AWAY FROM YOUR FRIEND EMMA, THE MORE **INTERESTED** SHE **GETS!** **YOU** KNOW HOW LOIS IS!

YEAH, I **DO** KNOW HOW LOIS IS! THE AVERAGE LENGTH OF HER RELATIONSHIPS IS **THREE NIGHTS!** I JUST DON'T WANT EMMA TO GET **HURT.**

I DUNNO, JEZ. EMMA SOUNDS LIKE SOMEONE WHO CAN TAKE CARE OF HERSELF.

MAYBE. THE OTHER THING IS, I JUST DON'T WANNA GET STUCK IN THE **MIDDLE,** Y'KNOW? I'M TOO OLD FOR THIS **EMOTIONAL TUG-OF-WAR** STUFF.

OH. YEAH, I FORGOT, YOU'RE FRIENDS WITH EMMA'S **HUSBAND,** TOO.

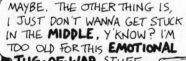

AFTER ALL, I KNEW JEROME **FIRST.** WHEN I GOT TO COLLEGE I'D NEVER **MET** A BLACK ACTIVIST BEFORE. HE **POLITICIZED** ME! AND IT WAS THROUGH HIS CLASSES THAT I EVENTUALLY **CAME OUT.** I JUST FEEL A CERTAIN **LOYALTY** TO HIM.

67

Swept Away

© 1989 BY ALISON BECHDEL

⑤3

LOIS TAKES A QUICK BREAK FROM THE BOOKSTORE...

GOOD COFFEE, HUH?

LOIS, I THINK YOU'RE A VERY ATTRACTIVE WOMAN AND I'D LIKE TO SLEEP WITH YOU.

GAK!

AHEM! YOU DON'T—COFF—**FOOL AROUND**, DO YOU?

NO, BUT I'D **LIKE** TO.

UM, JEEZ, EMMA... I'D LIKE TO SLEEP WITH YOU TOO... I'M JUST NOT USED TO WOMEN BEING SO **DIRECT**, Y'KNOW? I MEAN, THERE ARE CERTAIN **FORMALITIES** WE USUALLY GO THROUGH!

I DIDN'T MEAN TO SHOCK YOU. IT'S JUST THAT I'VE SPENT SO MUCH OF MY LIFE DOING THINGS FOR OTHER PEOPLE...NOW THAT I KNOW WHAT I REALLY **WANT**, I DON'T WANT TO WASTE ANY **TIME**.

EVERY MOMENT IS **PRECIOUS.**

UH... JEZANNA MENTIONED SOMETHING ABOUT YOU HAVING A **HUSBAND** AND **TWO KIDS**...

YES, JEROME AND I HAVE JUST SEPARATED. MY KIDS ARE **12** AND **18.** JAMES IS STAYING WITH HIS FATHER AND AMELIA IS AWAY AT SCHOOL. **SHE'S** A LESBIAN **TOO.**

UH-HUH, RIGHT. I DUNNO, EMMA... I SUDDENLY FEEL LIKE I'M IN A **PLAY.** ARE YOU FOR **REAL?**

I'M JUST BEING **HONEST,** LOIS. I DON'T HAVE TIME FOR GAMES. SO HOW ABOUT **FRIDAY NIGHT?**

UH... FINE, OKAY.

7 O'CLOCK, DINNER AT MY NEW APARTMENT? HERE'S THE ADDRESS. I HOPE **PIZZA'S** OKAY. I'M NOT SET UP TO COOK YET.

7 O'CLOCK. SURE... UM... SEE YOU THEN?

I'LL BE COUNTING THE HOURS. BYE-BYE.

AFTER the FACT

54

THAT WAS REALLY NICE, LOIS.

SO, HAVE I **CONVERTED** YOU?

WELL...IF I HADN'T DECIDED TO CONVERT BEFORE I EVEN **MET** YOU, YOU JUST MIGHT HAVE.

YEAH? WOW. CAN I HAVE A CIGARETTE?

NO. SMOKING IS A **TERRIBLE** HABIT.

LISTEN, YOU MAY BE **OLDER** THAN ME, BUT YOU'RE **NOT** MY MOTHER.

YOU'RE ABSOLUTELY RIGHT. I DON'T KNOW WHAT I WAS THINKING. HERE.

NO THANKS.

IT'S JUST... I'VE NEVER **CARED** SO MUCH IF SOMEONE CALLED ME OR **NOT**, Y'KNOW? I FEEL KIND OF **CRAZY**.

WHY ARE YOU SO CONVINCED SHE'S NOT GOING TO CALL?

I JUST **FEEL** IT, SOMEHOW. AFTER WE MADE LOVE, SHE WAS IN SUCH A HURRY TO GET RID OF ME.

MAYBE SHE WANTED TO BE **ALONE** TO PROCESS THE EXPERIENCE...

AFTER ALL, SLEEPING WITH A WOMAN FOR THE FIRST TIME IS KIND OF A BIG DEAL.

YEAH... MAYBE THAT WAS IT.

MAYBE SHE WAS EXPECTING SOMEONE ELSE **AFTER** YOU, SO SHE'D HAVE A BASIS FOR **COMPARISON**!

MO!

I COULDN'T RESIST.

FIX IT UP!

56

As LOIS AWAITS A CALL FROM HER BELOVED...

IF ANYBODY PHONES WHILE I'M IN THE SHOWER, COME GET ME!

THINGS DEVELOP APACE IN THE TROUBLED CONJUGAL LIFE OF CLARICE & TONI!

I SENSE SOME HOSTILITY, TONI.

...s University

SCHOOL of SOCIAL WORK

ANA SANTIAGO
CLINICAL SOCIAL WORKER

HOSTILITY?! HOW ABOUT MURDEROUS WRATH? I'VE BEEN BETRAYED, LIED TO, MADE A FOOL OF! WHAT AM I SUPPOSED TO DO, KISS AND MAKE UP?

CLARICE, WHAT DOES THIS BRING UP FOR YOU?

HUH?

WHAT ARE YOU FEELING RIGHT NOW?

UM... LIKE I WISH I WAS SOMEWHERE ELSE.

WELL, AT LEAST SHE'S BEING HONEST! **THAT'S** A MAJOR BREAKTHROUGH!

TONI, I SUPPORT YOU BEING IN TOUCH WITH YOUR **RAGE** BUT LET'S TRY AND KEEP OUR COMMENTS CONSTRUCTIVE.

I FEEL LIKE YOU'RE BOTH **GANGING UP** ON ME! SO I SLEPT WITH SOMEONE ELSE! IT WAS JUST A FLING! I **LOVE** YOU, TONI!

IT'S NOT JUST THAT YOU SLEPT WITH GINGER... IT'S THAT YOU DIDN'T **TELL** ME!

OH, IF I'D **TOLD** YOU, EVERYTHING WOULD'VE BEEN **HUNKY DORY**, HUH?

I THINK MAYBE THIS WOULD BE A GOOD TIME FOR US TO CLARIFY YOUR GOALS HERE. WHY DID YOU DECIDE TO COME TO THERAPY TOGETHER?

ISN'T THAT WHAT YOU **DO** WHEN YOUR RELATIONSHIP IS FALLING APART?

CAN'T YOU JUST **FIX** US?

WE'RE NOT TALKING **TOASTER OVENS** HERE. I'M AFRAID IT'LL BE JUST A TAD MORE COMPLICATED THAN THAT...

75

HELL HOUSE 58

©1989 BY ALISON BECHDEL

AFTER AN EXHAUSTING DAY IN THE **SNAKE PIT** OF ACADEME, OUR INTREPID PH.D. CANDIDATE GINGER RETURNS TO THE **SISTERLY BOSOM** OF HER COLLECTIVE HOUSEHOLD FOR RESPITE AND SUSTENANCE.

AM I BEAT! I CAN'T WAIT TO COLLAPSE IN FRONT OF MTV WITH A HUNK OF REHEATED LASAGNE!

DIGGER! HOW'S MY **GIRL**?! HOW'S MY LITTLE **PUP**?

YES! HI GIRL! HOWZA WITTLE PUPPY-WUPPY?! ...UH...OOPS..

...AN EXCELLENT WAY TO RECYCLE THEIR PATRIARCHAL SCUM!

SPARROW, WHAT'S GOING ON IN THE LIVING ROOM?

OH, LOIS'S GROUP IS PLOTTING THEIR NEXT ACTION. I THINK THEY WANNA PUT **CRUDE OIL** IN THE SPRINKLER SYSTEM AT EXXON HEADQUARTERS OR SOMETHING. TASTE THIS.

WHAT IS IT?

IT'S SORT OF **SOUP-LIKE**. I THREW SOME LEFTOVERS TOGETHER.

UGH!

YEAH... I GUESS THAT LASAGNE GAVE IT AN **ODD TEXTURE**.

OH, SPARROW! NOT THE **LASAGNE! NOW** WHAT AM I GONNA EAT?!

PLENTY OF SOUP HERE. GRAB A BOWL.

WHERE?! EVERY EATING VESSEL WE **OWN** IS IN THE **SINK!** THIS PLACE IS **DISGUSTING!**

DON'T LOOK AT ME. I JUST WASHED A BUNCH OF DISHES ON, UM ... TUESDAY.

AND WHY DIDN'T LOIS **TELL** ME THERE WAS A MEETING HERE?! ONE NIGHT A WEEK TO WATCH TV IS ALL I ASK, AND THE **LESBIAN ARMY** DESCENDS ON MY LIVING ROOM**!!**

OH. SPEAKING OF TELLING YOU THINGS, MY FRIEND MILKWEED IS COMING FOR A VISIT.

MILKWEED? WHAT KIND OF A NAME IS **MILKWEED?**

WELL, WHEN I FIRST MET HER SHE WAS **PHYLLIS**, BUT NOW SHE LIVES ON THIS LESBIAN FARM AND CALLS HERSELF MILKWEED MOONGARDEN.

OH, GREAT. HOW LONG'S SHE **STAYING?**

Y'KNOW, I FORGOT TO ASK.

79

the VISITATION

As we look in on our happy household, Sparrow's friend **MILKWEED** has arrived for a stay of **INDETERMINATE LENGTH.**

59

© 1989 BY ALISON BECHDEL

HI MILKWEED. DAMN! NO MESSAGES ON THE MACHINE... HAVE YOU BEEN HERE ALL DAY?

YEAH. SOMEONE CALLED EARLIER. IT MIGHTA BEEN FOR YOU. EMILY OR IRMA OR SOMETHING.

EMMA? WAS IT EMMA?!

PLEASE, PLEASE, **PLEASE** LET IT BE EMMA!

HMM... MAYBE. I WROTE IT DOWN ON A PIECE OF PAPER SOMEWHERE...

OH, RIGHT! I COULDN'T FIND ANY MATCHES SO I **LIT IT** AT THE STOVE TO BURN SOME **INCENSE!** Y'KNOW, IT MIGHT'VE BEEN FOR **GINGER** ANYWAY.

HI EVERYONE!

80

81

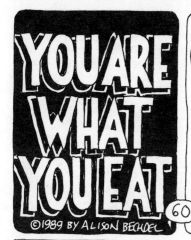

YOU ARE WHAT YOU EAT

©1989 BY ALISON BECHDEL

60

Our friend Milkweed is lurking in the kitchen when Lois has Mo over for dinner.

MILKWEED, YOU'RE WELCOME TO JOIN US IF YOU WANT.

THANKS! WHAT'RE YOU HAVING?

TUNAFISH-HIJIKI-ARUGULA CASSEROLE! IT'S MY OWN RECIPE.

TUNAFISH?! AT LEAST IT'S ALBACORE, I HOPE! DO YOU KNOW HOW MANY DOLPHINS ARE SLAUGHTERED ANNUALLY BY THE TUNA-FISHING INDUSTRY?

OH...YEAH, I HEARD SOMETHING ABOUT THAT.

WELL, I WOULDN'T HAVE IT ANYWAY... I DON'T EAT **FLESH**.

UM... THERE'S LEFTOVER **QUICHE** IN THE FRIDGE...

NO THANKS. I DON'T DO DAIRY.

82

83

Sermon on the Couch

61

© 1989 by Alison Bechdel

As the **TRUE NATURE** of our houseguest Milkweed unfolds, the patience of her hostesses is wearing **THIN!**

This morning, Sparrow & Ginger have already left for work and the **PHONE** is on its **THIRD RING**...

WHY ISN'T MILKWEED GETTING THAT?

DAMN! THE MACHINE'S NOT ON EITHER! WHAT IF IT'S **EMMA**?!

RING

DON'T HANG UP!

RING!

CLIK!

MILKWEED! WHY DINCHA ANSWER THE ☆#✦@✱ **PHONE?!**

SHHH! I'M MEDITATING!

That afternoon, a house meeting is called.

IT'S NOT JUST THE **TELEPHONE**, SPARROW! YESTERDAY SHE SPILLED HER ARTICHOKE-PAPAYA SMOOTHIE ALL OVER CHAPTER TWO OF MY **THESIS** WHILE SHE WAS 'BORROWING' MY TYPEWRITER!

85

Public **D**isplay of **A**ffection

62

© 1989 BY ALISON BECHDEL

MO AND HARRIET ARE PICKING UP A FEW PROVISIONS AT THE LOCAL SUPER-MARKET.

SHOP & DROP Megafoods

We're open INCESSANTLY!

Specials on ANTIBIOTIC-FED BEEF & IRRADIATED PRODUCE!

Save on PESTICIDES! ADDITIVES! PRESERV...

LET'S JUST GO **IN**, GET THE **STUFF**, AND GET **OUT**.

WHAT **ELSE** WOULD WE DO? I DIDN'T COME HERE TO **BROWSE**.

YANK!

I'M SORRY. THIS PLACE JUST FREAKS ME OUT. IT'S THE LIGHTING... OR THE SUBLIMINAL MESSAGES ON THE **MUZAK** URGING US TO EAT MORE **MEAT BY-PRODUCTS**.

JUST KEEP BREATHING AND YOU'LL BE OKAY.

SHOULD WE GET SOME FRUIT?

MMM... FRESH FIGS! KNOW WHAT THESE REMIND ME OF?

HARRIET!

WHAT?

WE'RE IN THE GROCERY STORE, FOR GODDESS' SAKE! COULD YOU, LIKE, DISENGAGE YOUR HAND FROM MY SHOULDER?

at the Salon

© 1989 BY ALISON BECHDEL

63

SO HOW'S YOUR LOVE LIFE, CASANOVA?

ROTTEN. I SEEM TO BE LOSING MY TOUCH.

NO LURID TALES OF SEDUCTION FOR ME THIS TIME?

NOT UNLESS YOU WANT TO HEAR ABOUT MY BREATHLESS NIGHTS SPENT PASSIONATELY WAITING FOR THE PHONE TO RING.

LO, THIS DOESN'T SOUND LIKE YOU! IS IT THE WOMAN YOU WERE DROOLING OVER LAST TIME? OLDER, MARRIED?

YEAH. WE HAD ONE DATE. PIZZA AND SEX ON HER FOLD-OUT COUCH.

HOW WAS IT?

SNIP!

WELL, I COULDA DONE WITHOUT THE ANCHOVIES, BUT SHE ORDERED BEFORE I GOT THERE.

89

The Option

After a surprise encounter at the hair salon, Lois has arranged to meet Emma following her appointment.

64

© 1989 By Alison Bechdel

SO. HOW 'BOUT THAT SUPREME COURT?

YEAH, REALLY. BAD NEWS.

YEAH.

LISTEN, I'M SORRY I NEVER CALLED.

OH THAT'S OKAY! IT'S NOT LIKE I WAS WAITING AROUND OR ANYTHING.

IT'S JUST THAT I'VE KIND OF GOTTEN INVOLVED WITH A GOOD FRIEND OF MINE.

OH.

I'VE BEEN IN LOVE WITH HER FOR OVER A YEAR. SHE'S WHY I FINALLY LEFT JEROME, BUT I DIDN'T KNOW HOW TO **APPROACH** HER... HOW TO GO ABOUT IT.

OH, **I** GET IT! SO YOU PRACTICED ON **ME** FIRST!

LOIS, NO...

Special vegetarian MEATLOAF w/steamed french fries

YEAH! THEN AFTER SLEEPING WITH **ME** YOU WENT AND SEDUCED YOUR FRIEND AND NOW YOU'RE BOTH MADLY IN LOVE. **SWELL**. GLAD I COULD HELP. AM I INVITED TO THE **WEDDING?**

LOIS, IT'S NOT LIKE THAT. YES, I FEEL A PRIMARY BOND WITH DOROTHY, BUT I'D LIKE TO SEE **YOU** NOW AND THEN TOO.

WELL ISN'T **THAT** PROGRESSIVE! OUT FOR TWO MONTHS AND ALREADY NONMONOGAMOUS!

WELL? ARE YOU INTERESTED OR NOT?

The SPAT

65

© 1989 By Alison Bechdel

LET ME GET THIS STRAIGHT. EMMA SAYS SHE'S INVOLVED IN A PRIMARY RELATIONSHIP WITH SOMEONE NAMED DOROTHY.

RIGHT.

BUT SHE'D LIKE TO SEE **YOU** ON THE SIDE.

WELL... I PREFER TO SAY "MORE CASUALLY."

LOIS, IF I LIKE SOMEONE SO MUCH I WANNA BE **INVOLVED** WITH HER, THEN I WANNA BE **INVOLVED** WITH HER, FER GODDESS' SAKE! NONE OF THIS "SECONDARY RELATIONSHIP" BULLSHIT!

I SAID **CASUAL**, NOT **SECONDARY**.

HOW CAN YOU EXCHANGE **INTIMATE BODILY FLUIDS** WITH SOMEONE AND CALL IT **CASUAL**?!

LISTEN! JUST BECAUSE YOU AND HARRIET INSTANTLY **MERGED IDENTITIES** DOESN'T MEAN THAT'S THE ONLY WAY TO DO THINGS!

93

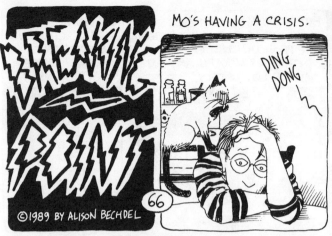

©1989 BY ALISON BECHDEL

66

MO'S HAVING A CRISIS.

DING DONG

HARRIET! THANK GOD YOU'RE HERE!

!

MO, WHAT'S WRONG!? DID SOMETHING HAPPEN?

I...I DUNNO! AT FIRST I THOUGHT I WAS JUST **PREMENSTRUAL**.. THEN I THOUGHT MAYBE IT WAS A **FOOD ALLERGY.** Y'KNOW, LIKE FROM THAT GLAZED DONUT I ATE MONDAY.

BUT NOW I THINK IT MUST BE MY **SATURN RETURN!**

WHAT IS? WHAT ARE YOU BABBLING ABOUT?!

MY **LIFE**, HARRIET! WHAT AM I DOING WITH MY **LIFE**?!

ALL THE YEARS OF BEING SOCIALLY **RESPONSIBLE**, STRUGGLING FOR **PEACE** AND **JUSTICE**, WORRYING MYSELF **SICK** ABOUT THE WORLD... WHERE HAS IT **GOTTEN** ME?

95

DRUG CULTURE

©1989 BY ALISON BECHDEL

67

MO'S NOT FEELING QUITE HERSELF LATELY.

HI, MO! C'MON IN. WE'RE WATCHING OUR FEARLESS LEADER JUST SAY NO.

HI, GANG.

UH-OH! REMEMBER THE **LAST** TIME YOU WATCHED A PRESIDENTIAL ADDRESS, MO? YOU REALLY BLEW A GASKET.

I'LL BE OKAY. I PROMISE I WON'T THROW ANYTHING THIS TIME.

SHH! LISTEN!

...BEEF UP LAW ENFORCEMENT... BUILD MORE PRISON SPACE...

RIGHT ON! THAT'S WHAT I'VE BEEN SAYING ALL ALONG! WHAT THIS NEIGHBORHOOD NEEDS IS A GOOD **JAIL!**

...AND TO COMBAT THE DRUG LORDS WHERE THEY LIVE, I PROPOSE SENDING 2 BILLION DOLLARS IN **MILITARY AID** TO COLOMBIA, PERU, AND BOLIVIA...

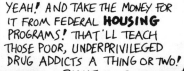

YEAH! AND TAKE THE MONEY FOR IT FROM FEDERAL **HOUSING** PROGRAMS! THAT'LL TEACH THOSE POOR, UNDERPRIVILEGED DRUG ADDICTS A THING OR TWO! RIGHT, MO?

DO YOU GUYS HAVE ANYTHING TO DRINK? I COULD GO FOR A CARBONATED BEVERAGE CONTAINING **CAFFEINE** AND **NUTRASWEET**.

WHAAT?

MO, ARE YOU OKAY?

...BLOCK BY BLOCK, CHILD BY CHILD...

MO! AREN'T YOU GONNA SAY ANYTHING ABOUT HOW BUSH IS **MANIPULATING** PEOPLE WITH **PATRIOTIC PLATITUDES**?!

OR HOW HE SHOULD DO SOMETHING ABOUT POVERTY AND RACISM **HERE** INSTEAD OF BLOWING UP SOUTH AMERICAN COUNTRIES?

SOME HIGHLY-PROCESSED, HEAVILY-SALTED **SNACK FOOD** WOULD ALSO HIT THE SPOT.

SHE FEELS A LITTLE FEVERISH.

WEIRD!

MO! AREN'T YOU EVEN GONNA POINT OUT THE **IRONY** OF A GUY WHO ONCE RAN THE **C.I.A.**, THAT **BASTION** OF COVERT DRUGS-FOR-ARMS DEALS, **PREACHING** AGAINST **CRACK**?

HEY, THIS GUY IS BORING. LET'S WATCH **MTV**.

INVASION OF THE BODY SNATCHERS...OR SATURN RETURN?! STAY TOONED!

Exclusive En-gagement

68

© 1989 BY ALISON BECHDEL

HOW ABOUT EARLY SPRING? OR JUNE! JUNE WOULD BE ROMANTIC!

OR WE COULD WAIT FOR OUR EIGHTH ANNIVERSARY AND DO IT THEN.

WILL YOU **STOP?** WE HAVEN'T DECIDED YET WHETHER WE'RE DOING IT AT **ALL.**

WELL **I'VE** DECIDED. I DON'T KNOW WHAT **YOUR** PROBLEM IS.

CLARICE, EXCUSE ME IF I SEEM **HESITANT.** ONE MINUTE YOU'RE HAVING AN AFFAIR AND **LYING** TO ME... THE NEXT, YOU WANT US TO DRESS UP IN **WHITE SATIN** AND SWEAR EVERLASTING **MONOGAMY** IN FRONT OF EVERYONE WE **KNOW.**

WILL YOU LET GO OF THE THING WITH GINGER? IT WAS **NOTHING!** DOESN'T THE FACT I'VE BEEN IN **THERAPY** WITH **YOU** FOR SIX MONTHS COUNT FOR ANYTHING?

ALL RIGHT. I'M SORRY. BUT WHY THE SUDDEN URGE TO GET **MARRIED?** A CEREMO-NY WON'T MAKE US MORE COMMITTED THAN WE ALREADY ARE.

99

It's Jezanna's annual coming out party, and the gang's all here!

©1989
69
BY ALISON BECHDEL

Well, Mo... you came out to your parents last year. What's your **NEXT STEP** gonna be?

Aw, Jez, I'm sick & tired of coming out! Life's hard enough without having to tell the **PLUMBER** you're a lesbian. Why knock ourselves out?

Because every time you **DON'T** come out, you let someone go on thinking they don't know any gay people! It makes us **INVISIBLE!**

But it's nobody's business who I sleep with! It's a **PERSONAL MATTER!**

Pretty to think so! But in this culture you're **PRESUMED** to be sleeping with the **OPPOSITE SEX** until proven otherwise!

Don't waste your breath, Jez. She's going through some weird **REACTIONARY PHASE.** Frankly, I'm worried. She just let her **GREENPEACE** membership lapse, and subscribed to **MS.** instead.

Think of it, Toni! What better way to come out to our families than by announcing our **COMMITMENT CEREMONY!**

101

THE DECISION

Mo HAS GROWN CONCERNED ABOUT THE STRANGE **DULLNESS** OF HER **ONCE ASTUTE** POLITICAL SENSIBILITIES!

(70)

© 1989 BY ALISON BECHDEL

OKAY. GO AHEAD. I'M READY.

THIS IS A GOOD ONE. IT SAYS HERE OLIVER NORTH MIGHT RUN FOR CONGRESS. DOES THAT GIVE YOU CHILLS OR WHAT?

UH-UH. TRY SOMETHING ELSE.

HOW 'BOUT THIS? EXXON SAYS PRINCE WILLIAM SOUND IS ALL CLEANED UP, AND THEY'VE STOPPED WORK BECAUSE IT'S GETTING COLD OUT.

NOPE. I STILL DON'T FEEL **ANYTHING.**

OKAY. THIS ONE'LL GET YOU. THE SPACE PROBE **GALILEO**, JUST LAUNCHED BY NASA, IS LOADED WITH ENOUGH **PLUTONIUM** TO KILL EVERYONE ON THE **PLANET.**

THE DANGER OF CONTAMINATION FROM THE PROJECT WON'T END TILL **1992**, AFTER THE PROBE WHIZZES BACK PAST EARTH AT A HEIGHT OF 185 MILES AND A SPEED OF 30,000 MILES PER HOUR.

DARN! I HAD A TWINGE OF **MILD CONCERN** FOR A SECOND THERE, BUT I LOST IT.

WHAT'S **WRONG** WITH ME? I'M **SCARED**!

YOU'RE SCARED? NEXT THING I KNOW YOU'LL BE VOTING **REPUBLICAN!** I MEAN, I LOVE YOU MO, BUT I HAVE TO DRAW THE LINE **SOMEWHERE.**

OKAY. THIS IS IT. TIME FOR **SERIOUS ACTION.** I'M GONNA **DO IT!**

WHAT? ORDER A **PIZZA?**

NO, HARRIET. I'M GOING TO CALL A **THERAPIST.**

WELL THAT'S GREAT, SWEETIE! I REALLY SUPPORT YOUR DECISION!

FINALLY!

JEEZ. THERE'S A LOT OF NAMES HERE! HOW WILL I EVER FIND THE RIGHT ONE? AND WHAT IF THEY'RE HOMOPHOBIC?

WHY DON'T YOU ASK ONE OF YOUR FRIENDS FOR SOME NAMES?

MAYBE THIS ISN'T SUCH A GOOD IDEA AFTER ALL. I THINK I WAS OVERREACTING. IN FACT, I FEEL BETTER ALREADY!

SENATOR OLIVER NORTH?

I'LL CALL SPARROW TOMORROW.

103

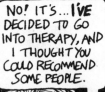

105

THE Quest

72

© 1989 BY ALISON BECHDEL

A COMPARISON SHOPPER BY NATURE, OUR HEROINE HAS BOOKED APPOINTMENTS WITH **THREE** DIFFERENT THERAPISTS THIS AFTERNOON!

"WHAT MODE OF DISCIPLINE DID YOUR PARENTS EMPLOY WITH YOU AS A CHILD?" JEEZ, I **HATE** FORMS!

MO?

INTAKE QUESTIONNAIRE, PAGE SIX.

UH...HI.

HERE, I'LL TAKE THOSE.

Impressive Credentials

GEETA SINGH, L.C.P.

HM.

UM...I'VE BEEN FEELING KINDA WEIRD LATELY...

I SEE HERE YOU DON'T HAVE ANY INSURANCE. DO YOU REALIZE A **50**-MINUTE SESSION COSTS $85?

SLIDING FEE? OF COURSE! I HOPE YOU DON'T MIND **SNAKES**! I BOUGHT HER YEARS AGO TO TREAT A PHOBIC CLIENT!

107

The Session

© 1989 BY ALISON BECHDEL

73

Daunted after three unsuccessful ventures, MO determines to try **ONE LAST THERAPIST.**

GREAT. THIS ONE'S LATE. IF SHE'S NOT HERE IN ONE MORE MINUTE, I'M BAGGING THE WHOLE DEAL.

AH! YOU MUST BE MO! SORRY I'M LATE! I WAS DOWNTOWN AT A DEMONSTRATION!

YOUR TAXES PAY FOR TORTURE, RAPE & MURDER IN EL SALVADOR

UNFORTUNATELY, WE DECIDED TO BLOCK TRAFFIC AT THE VERY INTERSECTION WHERE I'D PARKED MY CAR! HA HA! COME IN, COME IN!

YOU WERE AT THE EL SALVADOR DEMO? I DIDN'T THINK THERAPISTS DID STUFF LIKE THAT.

AH! WHAT KIND OF 'STUFF' DID YOU THINK WE **DO**?

UH... I DUNNO. PLAY BRIDGE. HAVE POTLUCKS. GO TO SEMINARS ON CODEPENDENCY. THAT SORT OF THING.

The MESSAGE

©1990 BY ALISON BECHDEL

75

MMM, EMMA... THOSE FISHSTICKS WERE **DELICIOUS**.

I'M SORRY... AFTER COOKING FOR MY FAMILY ALL THOSE YEARS, I JUST DON'T HAVE MUCH ENERGY TO PUT INTO IT ANYMORE.

HEY, I MEAN IT! I **LOVED** THEM! MY HAPPIEST CHILDHOOD MEMORIES ARE OF EATING FISH-STICKS IN FRONT OF THE **FLINTSTONES**.

YOU'RE SWEET. MMM... YOU **SMELL** SWEET TOO. WHAT IS THAT?

OH, A LITTLE OF THIS, A LITTLE OF THAT. EMMA, IT'S SO NICE TO BE ALONE WITH YOU AGAIN.

YOU TOO.

RING!

113

an Unusual Plight

© 1990 BY ALISON BECHDEL

76

Clarice and Toni are just returning from their support group for lesbians in **MULTICULTURAL RELATIONSHIPS.**

SHEESH! IF THAT'S SUPPORT, I DON'T THINK I EVER WANNA SEE **ANTAGONISM!**

OH, COME ON! EVERYONE WAS **VERY** SUPPORTIVE... EXCEPT **TANYA**, OF COURSE.

DO YOU THINK SHE'S RIGHT? ARE WE JUST MAKING A PATHETIC BID FOR APPROVAL FROM A RACIST, IMPERIALIST, MISOGYNISTIC, HETEROSEXIST SYSTEM THAT WANTS TO **DESTROY** EVERYTHING WE STAND FOR?!

CLARICE, TANYA SAID THE EXACT SAME THING ABOUT YOU GOING TO LAW SCHOOL AND ME BEING A **C.P.A.!** IT NEVER BOTHERED YOU BEFORE!

WELL YEAH, BUT...

OKAY. **WHAT** IS GOING ON?

114

115

resistance

HOW DID YOU **FEEL** WHEN YOUR MOTHER SAID YOU WERE TOO OLD TO BE KISSED GOODNIGHT?

ANYA MATUSZEWSKI, L.C.S.W.

77

© 1990 BY ALISON BECHDEL

LOOK, THIS IS **ABSURD!** I CAN'T BELIEVE I'M PAYING **GOOD MONEY** TO SIT HERE COMPLAINING ABOUT MY MIDDLE-CLASS, DR. SPOCK CHILDHOOD WHILE **HOMELESS** PEOPLE ARE STARVING IN THE **STREETS!** IT'S **IMMORAL!**

IMMORAL? WHY?

WHY?! LOOK OUT THE WINDOW, ANYA! WAR! RAPE! DRUG ABUSE! RACISM! WITH ALL THE **PAIN** IN THE WORLD IT'S **SELFISH** FOR ME TO SIT HERE WHINING ABOUT HOW MY MOTHER WOULDN'T KISS ME GOODNIGHT WHEN I WAS SIX!

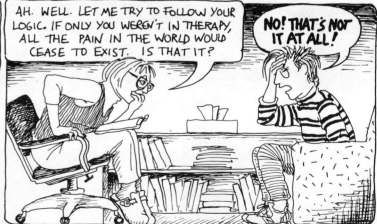

AH. WELL. LET ME TRY TO FOLLOW YOUR LOGIC. IF ONLY YOU WEREN'T IN THERAPY, ALL THE PAIN IN THE WORLD WOULD CEASE TO EXIST. IS THAT IT?

NO! THAT'S NOT IT AT ALL!

WILL MO'S WORLD-WEARY SHOULDERS FIND BALM IN THE **BOSOM** OF THE **PSYCHOTHERAPEUTIC PROCESS**? WILL LOIS AND EMMA SUCCESSFULLY NEGOTIATE THE TREACHEROUS WATERS OF **NON-EXCLUSIVITY**? WILL CLARICE AND TONI SOON BE COMPARISON SHOPPING FOR A **TURKEY BASTER**? ... AND WHAT ABOUT **NAOMI**?

DON'T TOUCH THAT REMOTE CONTROL!

Other titles from Firebrand Books include:

Artemis In Echo Park, Poetry by Eloise Klein Healy/$8.95

Before Our Eyes, A Novel by Joan Alden/$8.95

Beneath My Heart, Poetry by Janice Gould/$8.95

The Big Mama Stories by Shay Youngblood/$8.95

The Black Back-Ups, Poetry by Kate Rushin/$8.95

A Burst Of Light, Essays by Audre Lorde/$8.95

Cecile, Stories by Ruthann Robson/$8.95

Crime Against Nature, Poetry by Minnie Bruce Pratt/$8.95

Diamonds Are A Dyke's Best Friend by Yvonne Zipter/$9.95

Dykes To Watch Out For, Cartoons by Alison Bechdel/$7.95

Dykes To Watch Out For: The Sequel, Cartoons by Alison Bechdel/$9.95

Exile In The Promised Land, A Memoir by Marcia Freedman/$8.95

Experimental Love, Poetry by Cheryl Clarke/$8.95

Eye Of A Hurricane, Stories by Ruthann Robson/$8.95

The Fires Of Bride, A Novel by Ellen Galford/$8.95

Food & Spirits, Stories by Beth Brant (*Degonwadonti*)/$8.95

Forty-Three Septembers, Essays by Jewelle Gomez/$10.95

Free Ride, A Novel by Marilyn Gayle/$9.95

A Gathering Of Spirit, A Collection by North American Indian Women edited by Beth Brant (*Degonwadonti*)/$10.95

Getting Home Alive by Aurora Levins Morales and Rosario Morales/$9.95

The Gilda Stories, A Novel by Jewelle Gomez/$9.95

Good Enough To Eat, A Novel by Lesléa Newman/$8.95

Humid Pitch, Narrative Poetry by Cheryl Clarke/$8.95

Jewish Women's Call For Peace edited by Rita Falbel, Irena Klepfisz, and Donna Nevel/$4.95

Jonestown & Other Madness, Poetry by Pat Parker/$7.95

Just Say Yes, A Novel by Judith McDaniel/$9.95

The Land Of Look Behind, Prose and Poetry by Michelle Cliff/$8.95

Legal Tender, A Mystery by Marion Foster/$9.95

Lesbian (Out)law, Survival Under the Rule of Law by Ruthann Robson/$9.95

A Letter To Harvey Milk, Short Stories by Lesléa Newman/$9.95

Letting In The Night, A Novel by Joan Lindau/$8.95

Living As A Lesbian, Poetry by Cheryl Clarke/$7.95

Metamorphosis, Reflections On Recovery by Judith McDaniel/$7.95

Mohawk Trail by Beth Brant (*Degonwadonti*)/$7.95

Moll Cutpurse, A Novel by Ellen Galford/$7.95

The Monarchs Are Flying, A Novel by Marion Foster/$8.95

More Dykes To Watch Out For, Cartoons by Alison Bechdel/$7.95

Movement In Black, Poetry by Pat Parker/$8.95

My Mama's Dead Squirrel, Lesbian Essays on Southern Culture by Mab Segrest/$9.95

Normal Sex by Linda Smukler/$8.95

The Other Sappho, A Novel by Ellen Frye/$8.95

(continued)

Out In The World, International Lesbian Organizing by Shelley Anderson/$4.95

Politics Of The Heart, A Lesbian Parenting Anthology edited by Sandra Pollack and Jeanne Vaughn/$12.95

Presenting...Sister NoBlues by Hattie Gossett/$8.95

Rebellion, Essays 1980-1991 by Minnie Bruce Pratt/$10.95

Restoring The Color Of Roses by Barrie Jean Borich/$9.95

A Restricted Country by Joan Nestle/$9.95

Running Fiercely Toward A High Thin Sound, A Novel by Judith Katz/$9.95

Sacred Space by Geraldine Hatch Hanon/$9.95

Sanctuary, A Journey by Judith McDaniel/$7.95

Sans Souci, And Other Stories by Dionne Brand/$8.95

Scuttlebutt, A Novel by Jana Williams/$8.95

Shoulders, A Novel by Georgia Cotrell/$9.95

Simple Songs, Stories by Vickie Sears/$8.95

Skin by Dorothy Allison/$13.95

Spawn Of Dykes To Watch Out For, Cartoons by Alison Bechdel/$9.95

Speaking Dreams, Science Fiction by Severna Park/$9.95

Staying The Distance, A Novel by Franci McMahon/$9.95

Stone Butch Blues, A Novel by Leslie Feinberg/$10.95

The Sun Is Not Merciful, Short Stories by Anna Lee Walters /$8.95

Talking Indian, Reflections on Survival and Writing by Anna Lee Walters/$10.95

Tender Warriors, A Novel by Rachel Guido deVries/$8.95

This Is About Incest by Margaret Randall/$8.95

The Threshing Floor, Short Stories by Barbara Burford/$7.95

Trash, Stories by Dorothy Allison/$9.95

We Say We Love Each Other, Poetry by Minnie Bruce Pratt/$8.95

The Women Who Hate Me, Poetry by Dorothy Allison/$8.95

Words To The Wise, A Writer's Guide to Feminist and Lesbian Periodicals & Publishers by Andrea Fleck Clardy/$5.95

The Worry Girl, Stories from a Childhood by Andrea Freud Loewenstein/$8.95

Yours In Struggle, Three Feminist Perspectives on Anti-Semitism and Racism by Elly Bulkin, Minnie Bruce Pratt, and Barbara Smith/$9.95

You can buy Firebrand titles at your bookstore, or order them directly from the publisher (141 The Commons, Ithaca, New York 14850, 607-272-0000).

Please include $2.00 shipping for the first book and $.50 for each additional book.

A free catalog is available on request.

New, Improved! Dykes To Watch Out For, Cartoons by Alison Bechdel/$8.95